WILL SOLVIT

AND THE
AZTEC
EMPIRE OF
DOOM

PaRragon

Bath · New York · Singapore · Hong Kong · Cologne · Delhi · Melbourne

Written by Zed Storm
Creative concept and story by E. Hawken
Words by Rachel Elliot
Check out the website at www.will-solvit.com

First edition published by Parragon in 2010

Parragon
Queen Street House
4 Queen Street
Bath BA1 1HE, UK

ISBN 978-1-4454-0461-5

Printed in China

Please retain this information for future reference.

CONTENTS

Gross!

Tick! tock!

Tick! tock

Yuck!

CHAPTER ONE
LOCKER SHOCKER

I stared at the letter in my locker. It was such a shock to see it there that I felt frozen to the spot. I thought I was going to get a break from Adventures after my last one, but I guess not!

"Well open it then!" my best friend Zoe whispered excitedly in my ear.

I never knew where I was going to find these mysterious letters. (The last one had appeared on the attic floor at Grandpa's house, right after my Adventure in ancient Rome.) But I knew that finding a new letter was the start of something totally awesome.

You see, I come from a long line of Adventurers, and the letters always give me clues that help in my Adventures. Even though I don't have a clue who they are from, I've seen enough to know that I can completely trust them. And when you're an Adventurer, it pays to know who you can trust. Like Zoe, for example. She's totally trustworthy.

"Will, if you don't open it right now then I will!" she insisted.

Oh, yeah, and she can also be really bossy.

"I'll open it after school," I said, stuffing it into my pocket and shutting the locker door. "I don't want to open it here."

Adventuring has taught me a lot of things, but everyone must know that opening an interesting-looking letter in the middle of the school's main corridor is just asking for someone to snatch it.

"Will, you are so annoying!" Zoe sighed.

"I like you too," I replied, grinning at her.

She let out a little explosive noise and rolled

Girls can be _such_ a nightmare!

her eyes at me.

"OK, but don't go rushing off after school, will you? I'm dying to know what it says!"

I was dying to know what it said too. With any luck, it was going to lead me one step closer to finding my parents.

You see, I've been living with Grandpa Monty since Mum and Dad got stranded in a prehistoric jungle. I guess that sounds kind of weird, but it was all thanks to Morph, the amazing machine my dad invented. Morph can do incredible things, like turning into anything at all, or travelling through time. The trouble is, Morph doesn't always do what I expect . . . or what I want!

When I found out that I come from a long line of Adventurers, things really started to happen to me. I had some amazing Adventures travelling through time with Morph. I even met some of my ancestors. Each of them had been born with a special Adventuring skill. (I don't know what mine is yet, though, which is kind of annoying.)

The trouble is that for all the mind-blowing things I've seen and done, I can't forget that my parents are still trapped in time somewhere. I have to find them. That's the most important thing in the world to me. It's definitely more important than homework (I guess that's not saying much – most things are more important than homework).

Anyway, that was why I didn't take as much care over it as my teacher Mrs Jones wanted me to. And that was why she was looming over me at the start of the afternoon lesson.

"Will, this is NOT GOOD ENOUGH."

She really did say it in capital letters!

"It's a big disappointment after your wonderful essay on ancient Rome," she went on.

I could feel Zoe's eyes burning into the back of my head. She hates the fact that I ace tests about places I've time-travelled to!

"You obviously did very little research," Mrs Jones said. "And your handwriting is so messy that I could hardly read it. I've had to mark you down for that as well." She glared at me through her thick glasses. "Must do better, Will!"

"I don't know what her problem is anyway," I told Zoe after school, as we headed for the skate park. "My handwriting's fine. It's her eyesight that's 'NOT GOOD ENOUGH'."

"Get real. Your handwriting looks like a spider walked in some ink and then ran all over the paper," said Zoe.

Take it from me, never argue with Zoe. It's not

11

worth it – you will lose.

We dropped our backpacks in the corner of the park and sat down on our skateboards.

"Do you want to see what's in this letter or not?" I replied.

I was trying to sound cool and calm, but inside I was feeling mega-excited. I was really hoping that this would be the letter that would finally answer all my questions and lead me to my parents. I pulled out the envelope and ripped it open.

WHAT KIND OF CANS DO YOU FIND IN MEXICO? MEXICANS!

YOUR NEXT ADVENTURE WILL TAKE YOU TO A PLACE WHERE YOU ARE ALREADY EXPECTED.

• IT WAS A GREAT EMPIRE UNTIL IT WAS CONQUERED BY A SPANIARD NAMED CORTÉS.

- THE PEOPLE SPOKE A LANGUAGE CALLED N'AHUATL.
- THEY USED PICTURES AS AN ALPHABET INSTEAD OF LETTERS.

GOOD LUCK, WILL!

We were both silent for at least a minute while we tried to figure it out.

"OK," Zoe said eventually. "I give up. What does it mean?"

"Mexico," I murmured.

"I'll check those words online," Zoe stated.

I didn't reply. I was thinking about the clues I'd collected on my Adventures.

During my other Adventures, I had found proof that my father had invented another time machine, and my parents had left the prehistoric jungle where I lost them. I also know that they had been separated for some reason. The letters sometimes gave me clues about what had happened to them and I've started keeping a record of all the clues. One letter said that I should look for my mother in the past and my father in the future. From the sound of it, my next Adventure might lead me to my mother.

I jumped as Zoe bawled in my ear.

"What's the matter with you?" I yelped, rubbing my ear.

"I'd have thought an Adventurer would pay more attention to what was going on around him!" she said, waving her SurfM8 at me. "I've just checked 'N'ahuatl' out on the internet, and I know exactly where your next Adventure is going to be!"

"Where?" I cried in excitement.

"The ancient Aztec Empire!" she announced.

She sounded mega-triumphant, but

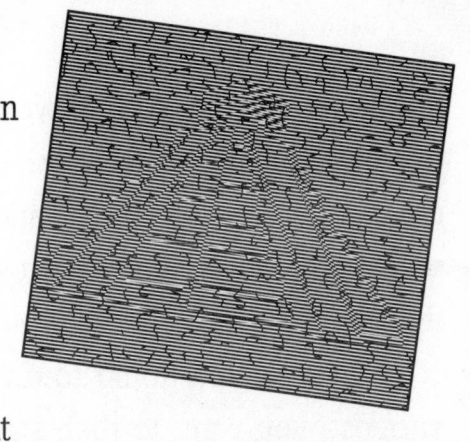

it was totally wasted on me. I had no clue what she was talking about. I must have looked a bit blank, cuz Zoe rolled her eyes and grinned at me.

"Mexico, hundreds of years ago," she said. "How cool is that?!"

"Brilliant," I said.

Zoe shot me a funny look. I was feeling a bit weird. One part of me couldn't wait to get home and see if Morph was ready to take me back into the past (I'd never heard of the Aztecs before and I was looking forward to finding out more).

But another part of me was worried. I'd had enough Adventures to know that they were completely unpredictable, and it was definitely weird that I was already expected. What did that mean?

"What are you going to do?" asked Zoe. "I suppose you want to rush straight off and jump into Morph?"

She was trying really hard not to sound disappointed, but I knew that she'd been looking forward to having a skate. The Aztec Empire would still be there later. I jumped onto my skateboard and grinned at my best friend.

"Come on," I said. "Bet you can't do a 'rock and roll' down the ramp!"

AWESOME!

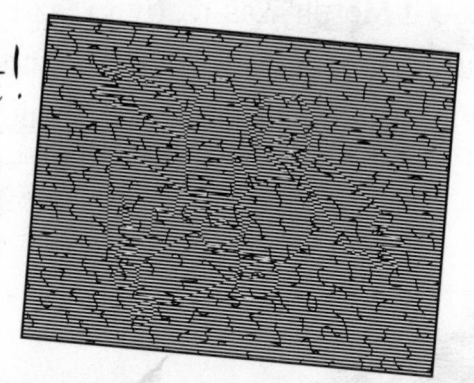

"There you are, Frederick!" Grandpa called from the kitchen.

This was a new one to me, but Grandpa hardly ever got my name right so I wasn't too worried. I dumped my backpack and skateboard in the hall, and then walked into the kitchen. Grandpa waved a piece of paper at me.

"News from Professor Locke and your little friend!" he said, chuckling.

That was Grandpa's idea of a joke. Professor Locke owns a remote island. He lives there with my friend Ned, who comes from the stone age, and my pet dinosaur, Rex. (Yep, that's

Roaaarrr!

17

right – my 'little friend' is a T-rex.) I was dying to tell Grandpa about the latest letter, but I wanted to know how Rex and the Professor were too. I reached into the biscuit jar and pulled out a grape and onion cookie. Grandpa is an experimental cook.

"Are they OK? How's Ned?" I asked.

I tried a bite of the cookie, choked and then dropped it on the floor for Grandpa's dog Plato. He sniffed it, licked it and then backed away and hid under Grandpa's chair.

"They're fine," said Grandpa. "Very well. Rex has only eaten a few of the other animals on the island, and Ned is learning something new about the twenty-first century every day." He looked down at the letter again. "Although it seems as though he already knew plenty about skateboarding. He's been teaching Professor

Locke a few moves."

I grinned. Ned had taken to skateboarding like a salmon takes to swimming.

"That's brilliant, Grandpa," I said. "Listen, I've got something to tell you. I found another let—"

"I haven't got time to listen to Adventure stories!" Grandpa exclaimed, struggling to his feet. "I've finally perfected my recipe for beef and ice-cream soup. All it needed was an extra teaspoon of peanut butter!"

He started rattling saucepans and opening cupboards.

"What do you know about the Aztecs, Grandpa?" I asked.

"Attics?" he said above the clatter of pans. "Dusty places, don't like them. Now, where did I put that garlic cream?"

There's no point talking to Grandpa when

he's creating a new recipe. I raced up to my room, where Morph was sitting on my desk in the shape of a miniature time machine. (Dad designed Morph to shrink down to a miniature version of whatever it was last used for when it's not in use.) But right now I didn't need a time machine – I needed a computer.

I searched through my memory chips to find the right program, then I put the chip in Morph and pressed my thumb down on the X-ray pad beside the disk drive. Morph let out a burst of blue sparks, gave a weird whistling sound and then morphed into a laptop.

"Fantastic," I said. "OK, Mrs Jones, I'll show you how good I am at research!"

I tapped the words 'Aztec empire' into a search engine and started surfing the web. There was a humongous amount of information about the

Aztecs – it was like wading through mud trying to figure out what was really important and what was just boring historical waffle.

While I was staring at the screen, the light outside faded. The smell of beef and ice-cream soup came wafting up the stairs . . . closely followed by the smell of burned beef and ice-cream soup. I vaguely heard Grandpa washing up and Stanley, Grandpa's driver, calling Plato to go for a walk, but I got kind of lost in the Aztec world I was reading about. Here are the top ten things I learned about the Aztec Empire:

1. Aztec is the overall name for various groups of people who lived in central Mexico in the fourteenth, fifteenth and sixteenth centuries.
2. The Aztec people were once travellers

called Mexicas, but their god sent them a sign and they started to build a city.

3. The city became one of the largest cities in the world. Their military power grew and they started to conquer other groups.

4. Each Aztec home had a steam bath.

5. An Aztec weapon could chop off the head of a horse with one blow.

6. The word chocolate comes from the Aztec word 'chocolatl'.

7. The Aztecs believed that they owed a blood-debt to the gods, so they sacrificed animals – and humans!

8. In a human sacrifice, the victim would lie on a stone slab. Their heart would be removed and held up to the sun. Then the body would be thrown down the stairs of the temple.

I am soooo glad I wasn't around in those days!

9. The Aztecs loved music and played drums, flutes, rattles, horns and trumpets. Music was one of the most important subjects at school.
10. The Aztec Empire was one of the first civilisations to educate everyone, no matter what gender or class they were. How cool is that?!

I jumped out of my chair, feeling a sort of electric current running through my blood. Another Adventure was on the way and now I couldn't wait to get started! But first I had to pick out some Adventure tools. During one Adventure, I had been stuck in the Stone Age with no tools at all, and there was no way I was going to let that happen again!

I pulled my Adventure backpack out from

under the bed. It was looking pretty old and battered. On my last Adventure, it had travelled across the ancient Roman Empire with me, and even though I had shoved it in the washing machine, it still had the air of a backpack that had seen life. I loved it!

I walked slowly around my room, picking up anything I thought I might need. I had brought all Dad's best inventions from our house when I went to live with Grandpa, and I was really glad to have them when I found out about being an Adventurer! I packed:

- Camouflage paint
- Grandpa's spy diary
- Bottle of truth serum
- Invisibility paint
- Morph's memory chips

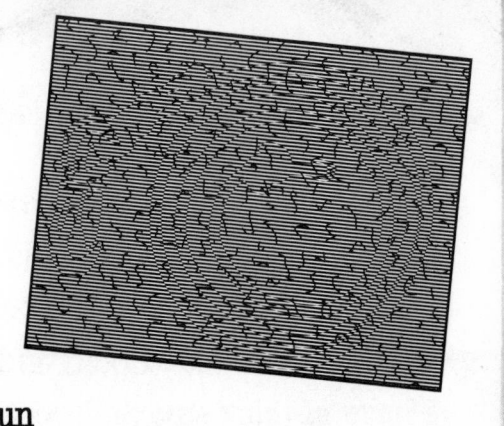

- Steel rope
- Pen that
  can write in
  any language
- Electric stun gun
- Compass that always points to home
- Memory obliterator
- Night-vision goggles
- My clue book

My backpack was filled to bursting point!

I stood in the middle of the room, my brain fizzing with thoughts. Who was expecting me in ancient times? What was I going to find out about my parents? Would Morph even allow me to time travel? Since being in the prehistoric jungle, Dad's incredible machine had been a bit moody.

I turned to the desk where I had left Morph

looking like a laptop. Suddenly Morph started to make a weird buzzing sound.

"Morph?" I said.

There was a loud ping and then Morph let out a haze of thick smoke. It made me cough and my eyes were stinging. I could hear Morph whirring and whizzing as if hundreds of cogs were turning at top speed.

When the smoke cleared and the noise stopped, Morph was no longer a laptop on my desk. Instead, a large time machine stood in the middle of the room.

"Brilliant!" I exclaimed.

Suddenly I had a thought. When I got back from my Stone Age Adventure, I found that I had been away for five weeks. That had been in the holidays, but this was term-time and the school would start asking questions if I disappeared for a month. I pulled out my SurfM8 and sent an IM to Zoe.

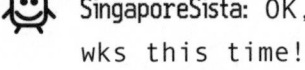

Wilz: I'm setting off!

SingaporeSista: Gd luck! Have u told yr Grandpa?

Wilz: Yes but he's busy wiv new recipe so not sure he'll remember!

SingaporeSista: LOL! Wot's the recipe?

Wilz: U dnt want 2 know! Can u do me a fvr?

SingaporeSista: Depends.

Wilz: If I'm not in school on Mon, cover 4 me?

SingaporeSista: OK, but it had btr not last wks this time!

Wilz: I'll do my best!

SingaporeSista: C U soon.

Wilz: Catch u l8r.

I shoved my SurfM8 back into my pocket, hoisted my backpack onto my shoulders and took a deep breath. Morph had fired up without me having to do a thing, and that meant just one thing – Adventure!

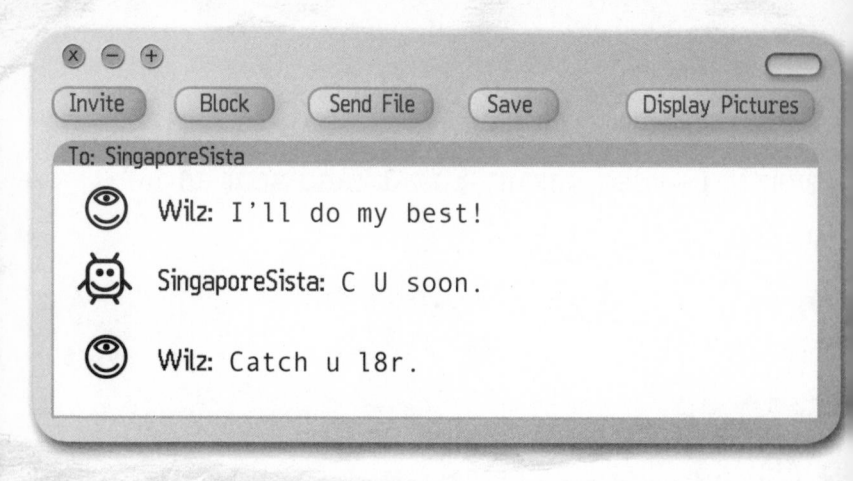

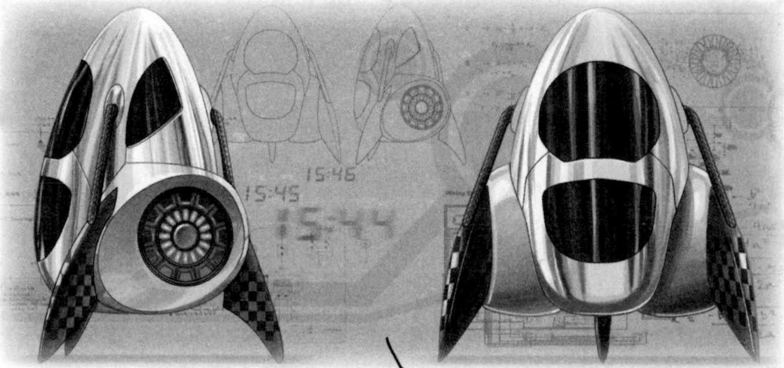

Totally cool!

28

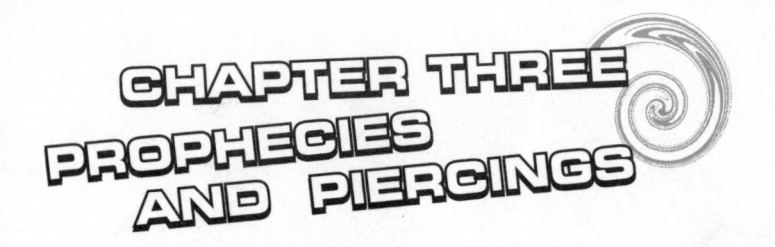
"WooHOO!" I yelled as I was thrown around inside Morph.

The journey had started even before I got the doors shut – Morph was really keen to get me there! It was like being inside a salt shaker. I shut my eyes and saw a swirl of colours. Then there was a hard jolt and I did a triple somersault through the air and landed on my bum.

"Ow!" I yelled. "Morph! Chill out, will you?"

I stood up, rubbing my backside, and peered out through the window. All I could see were thick green leaves. It reminded me of the jungle where I lost my parents. Had Morph taken me back there?

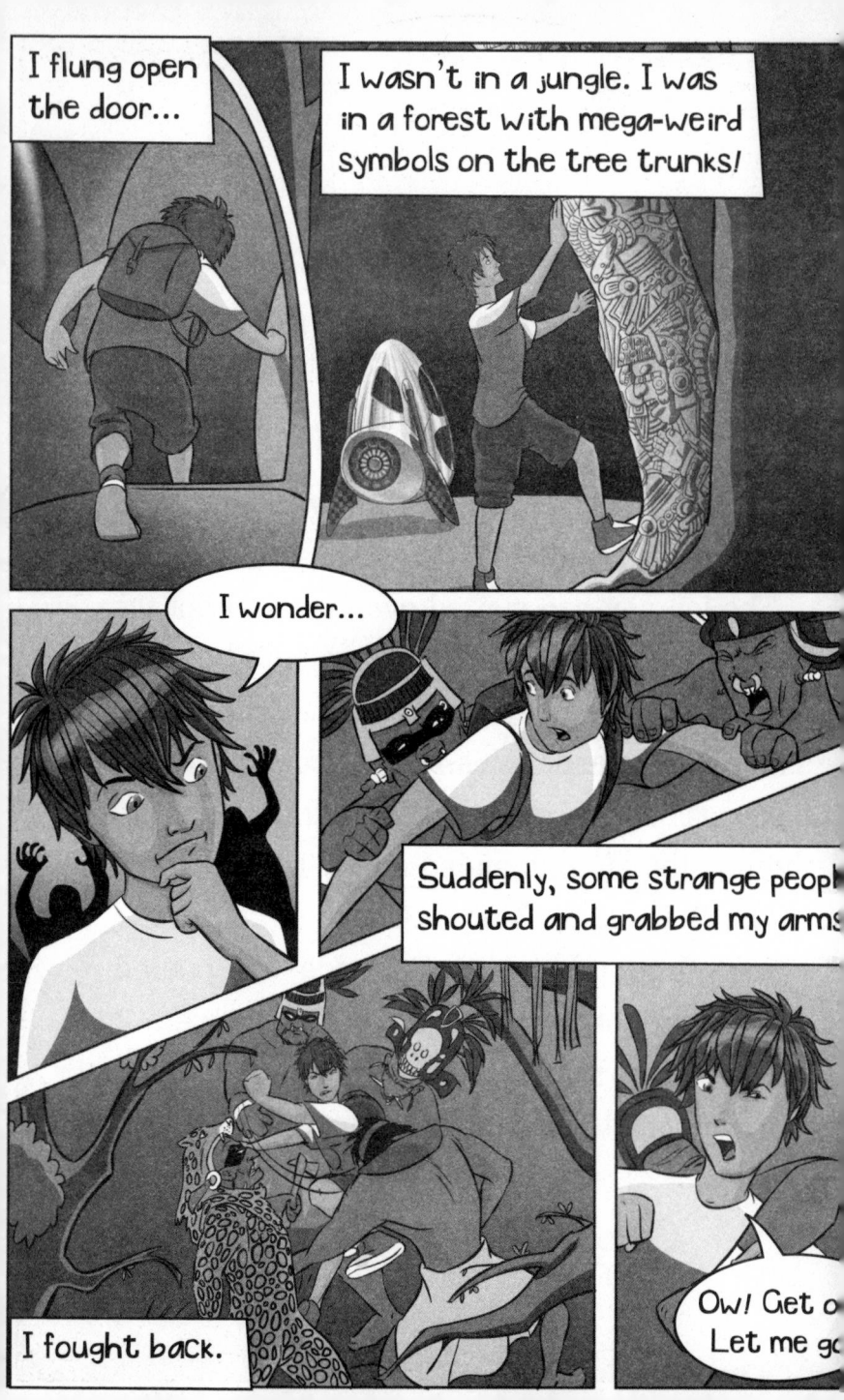

"We pay homage to the Master of Time!" said a man kneeling in front of me.

I didn't have a clue what he was talking about, but right then I didn't care – I couldn't stop staring at him. He looked brilliant! He was wearing animal furs draped over his shoulder like a toga, and his face was painted with strange patterns so I couldn't really tell what he looked like. He had a ton of piercings, but they were nothing like Zoe's ear piercings. His lips were pierced and decorated with gold discs and stones. His ears were so thickly pierced with gold that I could hardly see the skin, and there was a thick piece of stone through the central part of his nose – that had gotta hurt!

"Master?" said the man.

When he opened his mouth the discs hanging from his lips jangled, so music played whenever

This guy is total BLING!

he spoke. It was very cool but also mega
distracting.

"Sorry," I said, dragging my eyes away from
the fascinating piercings. "Hang on, what did you
call me? I'm not your master."

"You are the Master of Time," said the man.
"Your coming has been foretold for generations. It

is the single greatest prophecy of our people."

Now, as an Adventurer I'm getting used to weird stuff, but this was really spooky.

"I am Matlal, the King's chief advisor," the man said. "It is my honour to have been chosen as spokesman on this magnificent day of days."

He lay down flat on his face again.

I had to put a stop to all this. It was making me feel mega-weird. On my Adventures, I had got more used to people trying to kill me than people wanting to bow down to me!

"Listen," I said, "I wish you'd all stand up. I'm not a master of anything!"

I saw some of them looking at each other, but no one moved.

"Matlal, please," I said. "I don't even know why I'm here. I've got a ton of questions but I can't talk to you when you're face down on the ground!"

Matlal was a tall, broad-shouldered man. He suddenly stood up and the others copied him. Now I could see that they all had painted faces and piercings. Each man carried a spear that was as tall as him, and the spear tips gleamed in the sunlight. They looked deadly sharp.

"Ask your questions, Master," said Matlal.

"Thanks," I said. "And please, call me Will, OK?"

Matlal nodded his head once, very slowly. His expression was still and watchful, but when I looked into his eyes I could see amazement flickering there.

"Right," I said. "First question – have I come to the right place? Are you the Aztecs?"

"We have never heard that name," Matlal replied, looking puzzled.

I suddenly remembered something else I had read on the internet. People only started calling them the Aztecs hundreds of years after the Aztec Empire existed. At the time they were just known as 'Mexicas' and the Empire was called the 'Triple Alliance'.

"The Triple Alliance?" I said, hoping that I had remembered it right.

"That is what some people call it," Matlal agreed.

"So how come you knew where to wait for me?" I asked.

"The legend of Will Solvit has been told for generations," Matlal explained. "It was the first story I ever heard, sitting by the fireside as a tiny child. My grandfather told me about the Master of Time."

"Mine too," said one of his companions. "My

grandmother told me the legend. She was full of envy that it would happen during my lifetime. But I never imagined I would be here to witness the great moment in person!"

He looked as if he was going to start bowing again, so I spoke quickly. "That's great, but I still don't understand what the legend actually says."

"The legend stated exactly where and when you would appear," said Matlal. "It gives your name, and it says that you are the only one who can save us!"

The others nodded, muttering and thumping their spears on the ground in a sort of drum beat.

My brain felt as if someone had wrapped it up in cotton wool. None of this made sense to me! How could my name have been passed through generations as an Aztec legend? I hadn't even been born yet!

This is TOO weird!

"Save you from what, exactly?" I asked.

Why did I get the feeling that I wasn't going to like his answer?

"Death and destruction, Master," said Matlal, his voice shaking with emotion.

What is it about Adventures? I wondered as I looked at Matlal. Are they always life-threatening, or is it just that Morph likes to land me in the middle of trouble?

"Look, I'm really sorry," I said as gently as I could, "but I don't know anything about this legend. It's all some massive mistake."

"No mistake," said Matlal. "We have complete faith in the legend. You will not let us down."

I don't think he meant to sound sinister. I guess it's hard to smile when your lips are full of gold piercings. But his words sent goosebumps running up and down my back like ants. All my instincts were telling me to fire up Morph and get home as fast as I could, but I knew Morph wouldn't let that happen. Judging by my past Adventures, I'd be stuck here until Morph decided it was time to go.

"OK," I said. "You'd better tell me what's going on."

"Our King will do that," said Matlal. "He is waiting for you in the city. He will tell you all about Mutex."

His voice lowered to a hiss when he said the name, and the goosebump-ants set off on another sprint up and down my back.

"What is Mutex?" I asked, not sure that I was ready to hear the answer.

"The King will tell you everything," Matlal repeated. "Follow us, Master. We will lead you to the city . . . and then you will lead us to victory!"

The other men cheered and roared, waving their spears above their heads.

"Will Solvit! Will Solvit!" they chanted.

Yep, I was right. I definitely didn't like the sound of this.

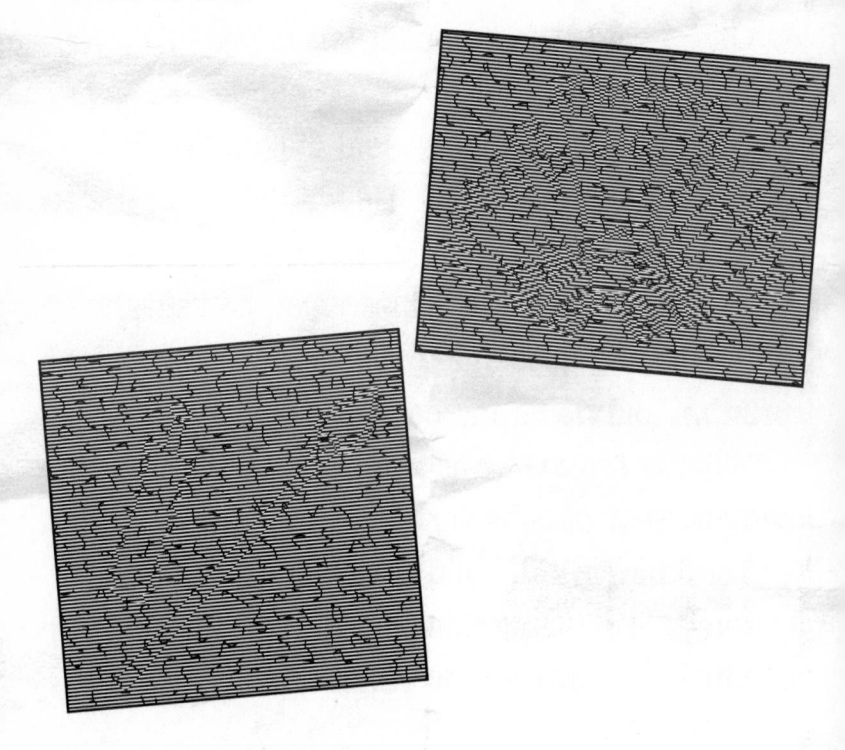

CHAPTER FOUR
KING OF THE AZTECS

After a short but fast march through the dense jungle, we arrived in a small, beautiful city. The stone of the buildings was so smooth and light, it seemed to shine like silver in the sunlight. But there was no time to look at all the incredible buildings. Matlal sped on to the central palace, and soon I was bowing to Cocoza, the King of the Aztecs.

I had thought that Matlal looked like a fearsome warrior, but next to King Cocoza he looked about as fearsome as a kitten. Every centimetre of Cocoza's tanned, sinewy body was decorated with battle scars and tribal tattoos. His many gold piercings were so jewel-encrusted that it was a miracle he could even stand up. He wore a kind of armour decorated with complex emblems, and in the centre of his chest was a picture of an eagle eating a snake.

"Your Majesty," I said, after finishing my bow. "I know you've been expecting me, but there's got to be some kind of a mistake. I'm not a warrior or anything – I'm just a kid!"

"The ancient manuscripts foretold that our saviour would be a child," said the King.

His deep, rich voice seemed to roll around the palace chamber where we stood, and echo out through the glassless windows.

"What ancient manuscripts?" I asked. "Can I see them?"

Perhaps these writings would give me some explanation for what was going on!

"By all means," said King Cocoza. "It was my intention to take you to see them. Come."

He strode out of the chamber and I followed. I had to run to keep up with him, because every one of his steps was about three of mine. He led me out of the palace and into the grounds. As we walked (and ran), I kept glancing sideways at him. He didn't talk much and, like Matlal, he never smiled. All those lip piercings made the Aztecs look fearsome, but I'd rather look less scary and be able to grin when I wanted to!

The palace grounds were amazing. King Cocoza pointed out two zoos, as well as an aquarium and beautiful botanical gardens. He sounded very proud of his home.

The palace was in the centre of the city, inside a walled square. As we walked further out, I saw masses of temples, schools and public buildings.

I soon figured out that the city was built beside a vast lake, and I saw dozens of canals lacing their way through the city.

There was something weird going on. For such a huge place, there weren't that many people about. I thought back to my visit to ancient Rome. There it had been impossible to walk in a straight line down any street – you were always getting shoved by other people. But here the streets weren't busy and it was quiet enough to be able to hear our footsteps on the stone slabs. I didn't see any children at all, so I guessed they were all in school. There were plenty of jungle animals roaming the streets, though! Wild monkeys clambered on the buildings, and tapirs and

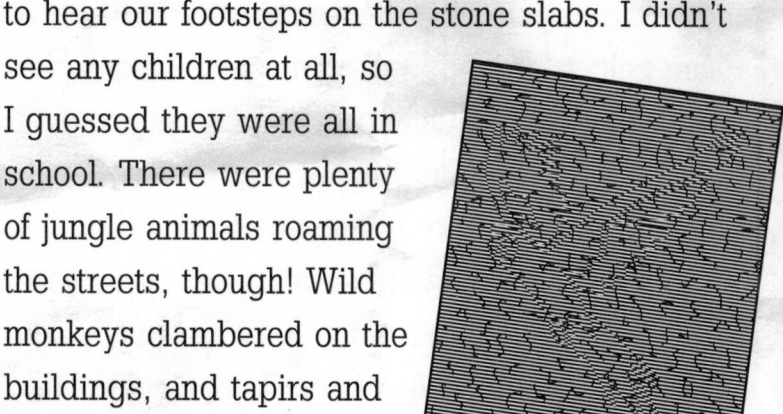

wild pigs snuffled at the ground. Parrots flew low over our heads.

"Why are the animals coming into the city?" I asked. "Is that normal here?"

"It is now," said the King, looking sad. "Where there are few humans, the animals grow bold. We have guards on constant watch for jaguars."

He stopped in front of a large temple. "We are here," he said. "In the centre of this temple lies a secret room, and that is where we keep the ancient manuscripts."

He led me up the wide stone steps and into the shade and cool of the temple. Our footsteps echoed loudly. At the centre of the temple was a large, square block made of stone, about the size of my bedroom at Grandpa's house. It reminded me of the design of the city, with the palace at the centre.

King Cocoza pressed one of the stones, and there was a loud groaning sound as three blocks slid sideways to make a door. A burning torch was clipped to the wall and the King took it down to light our way. A very short corridor led to a large, square table. Upon the table was a pile of ancient paper.

"These are the manuscripts," said the King. "Take a seat. They are impossible to read unless you have been trained, for the writing is strange and old. I have sent for a special scholar to come and read them to you."

"There's no need," I told him, peering at the paper in the flickering light. "I can read these, no problem."

This time I didn't need the amulet to translate for me – the script was modern, and it was

written in words that I would use. It even looked
like my handwriting! Weird! I read through
the papers as fast as I could, and then leaned
back and closed my eyes, my mind fizzing with
confusion. There was no doubt that these ancient
manuscripts were all about me. The writer knew:

- When and where I would appear.
- The fact that my time machine is
  called Morph.
- My age and appearance.

The writer also wrote that:

- I would defeat Mutex.
- I would lead an army into battle.
- I would possess a great treasure.

This was so super-strange that I even started to wonder if I was dreaming!

"I see this has come as a surprise to you," said King Cocoza.

That was the understatement of the century!

"You must understand that for as long as we can remember, we have known the legends of the Master of Time defeating Mutex," the King went on.

"But I still don't know what Mutex is," I said.

"Mutex is a man," replied the King. "At least . . . he was a man once. But many, many years ago, back in the mists of time, he stole something from my ancestor – the first King."

"What did he steal?"

King Cocoza looked weary.

"Mutex stole a sacred mask," he said. "A mask of such power and magic that even the gods would be envious of it."

"What does it do?" I asked.

"It makes the wearer invincible," said the King. "Try to imagine what that means. He cannot be killed when he is wearing it. He cannot be hurt or defeated or outwitted. He is immortal and unstoppable. He is a god in human form!"

I began to understand. Someone who had that sort of power would be able to do anything he wanted. If he was a bad man . . .

"Mutex is pure evil," said the King, as if reading my mind. "He uses the mask for destruction and control. For generations he has stolen our children in order to work for him. Now he plans to build a new city that will be ruled only by him. He has used the mask to control the minds of weak guards, promising them riches and power if they help force the children to work."

I thought of the empty city streets and the absence of children. They hadn't been in school – they had been abducted!

"What sort of work do the children have to do?" I asked, horrified.

"It is back-breaking, spirit-crushing work," said King Cocoza, his face twisting with emotion. "Some children are forced to cut down trees, stripping the jungle of its beauty, destroying the homes of the wild animals."

"Is that why the animals come here?" I asked.

The King nodded. "Other children are digging underground systems for the new city, or working as miners deep in the earth, searching for gold and turquoise. When Mutex's little slaves collapse from hunger or exhaustion, he just steals more children. He has a heart of stone."

"Don't any of them escape?" I asked.

Grrrrr! That makes me so mad!

50

"A few," the King answered, his eyes burning. "I was one of them."

The thought of the enslaved children made me feel sick. I couldn't turn away from this – I was needed. Somehow, I had to find a way to defeat Mutex.

Just then an elderly man appeared in the entrance to the secret chamber. I guessed that he was one of the King's special scholars. He bowed low.

"Your Majesty," he said in a cracking, reedy voice. "The games planned in honour of the Master of Time are ready to begin!"

CHAPTER FIVE
BLOODTHIRSTY
BASKETBALL

Now, I should explain that I've seen some
gruesome stuff in my time as an Adventurer.
I've seen the Romans shouting for blood in the
Colosseum. I've seen cannibal cavemen ravenous
for human flesh. I've even seen a T-rex popping
a small dinosaur like a balloon. But I have never
experienced anything quite so violent as the
Aztec version of basketball.

The game was played in a large courtyard
in the palace grounds. At first, I thought I was
going to enjoy it. The walls of the courtyard were
decorated with religious texts, and the basketball
hoops were made of gold that gleamed in the

sunlight. The players were painted and tattooed in their team colours – green and gold. I sat next to King Cocoza, so I had the best view – and trust me, that wasn't exactly good news!

There was no referee, and the players pushed, shoved and kicked each other to get the ball to the hoop. It seemed as if anything was allowed as long as they won!

A favourite method of getting the ball seemed to be to tug on the opposing player's piercings until they screamed in pain. Blood sprayed around the court and splattered anyone sitting in the front rows. Snarls of rage came from the players as they battled towards the hoops. I decided to concentrate on the ball instead.

I squinted at it, wishing I had a pair of binoculars with me. The ball looked as if it had something painted on one side.

"They're definitely . . . eye-catching," I said.

"They act as a warning to anyone who wages war on us or breaks the law," said the King.

"I bet it works," I muttered.

Before the King could reply, a tremor ran through the courtyard – a sort of ripple under the ground.

I had never felt an earthquake before that. I had only ever seen them in films or heard about them on the news. But I was pretty sure that where there was an earthquake, there was usually danger. I jumped up in a panic, but no one else moved or seemed at all worried.

"What was that?" I gasped.

"We have many of these shakes nowadays," said the King, with a little shrug. "I think the city is angry that we have not yet defeated Mutex and brought the children home."

I looked up at the jungle-covered mountains that surrounded the city and thought about what King Cocoza had told me. I thought about the hundreds of children working themselves to death underground, burrowing into the earth like animals. My stomach churned. It wasn't just the children who were in danger – it was every man, woman, child and animal who lived beside the mountains.

"I hate to disagree with you, Your Majesty," I said, "but this has nothing to do with the city being angry. This is all Mutex's doing. There is too much mining in those mountains, and too many underground tunnels. The mountains are starting to collapse in on themselves!"

The colour drained from the King's face. It felt weird to have a grown-up – and a King – believe every word I said so quickly. On most of my Adventures I seemed to spend ages trying to persuade people to listen to me! I could see that he felt helpless, and I rested my hand on his shoulder.

"I need to go," I said. "If I don't start looking for a way to defeat Mutex, your civilisation will disappear." (I was secretly happy to have a reason to get away from the game and all those heads anyway!)

King Cocoza stood up and grasped my forearm – the Aztec version of a handshake, I guess.

"Good luck, Master of Time Will Solvit," he said. "May good fortune ride with you, and may the winds always be at your back."

I walked away from the courtyard with the cheers of the crowd ringing in my ears. I wandered into the botanical gardens, looking for a good, quiet place to fire up Morph. I wanted to forget all about those gory heads on spikes. Time-travelling into the past is nothing like reading a history book or seeing pictures in a museum. I can still remember the smell of the stale blood.

I was heading towards a secluded square when I saw something white on the ground in front of me, and I pounced on it, my heart hammering against my ribs. It was another letter! I tore open the envelope as fast as I could.

WHY DO BASKETBALL PLAYERS LOVE COOKIES? BECAUSE THEY CAN DUNK THEM!

YOU CAME TO THE RIGHT PLACE, WILL. THE FUTURE OF THE AZTECS DEPENDS ON YOU! BUT NOW YOU NEED TO GO BACK TO THE START OF THE PROBLEM.

"The start of the problem," I read aloud.

What was that supposed to mean? What was the start of the problem?

Suddenly the truth hit me like an Aztec basketball between the eyes. Of course! I had to travel even further back in time – I had to go to the moment when Mutex first stole the mask. Perhaps the letter was telling me that I had a chance to stop the robbery!

I pulled Morph out of my backpack and fired up the time machine. As I stepped inside, I felt a moment of panic. How was I supposed to know where to go? I didn't even know the first King's name! But Morph's control panels began to flash, there was a shudder and a flash of red sparks, and then the doors slammed shut as Morph started to shake. Green squiggles flashed across the screen and I knew that I was being catapulted further and further back in time. Morph whizzed and clunked and we went faster and faster . . . and then stopped with a sickening lurch. We had arrived! But where were we? I pushed open the doors and stepped outside.

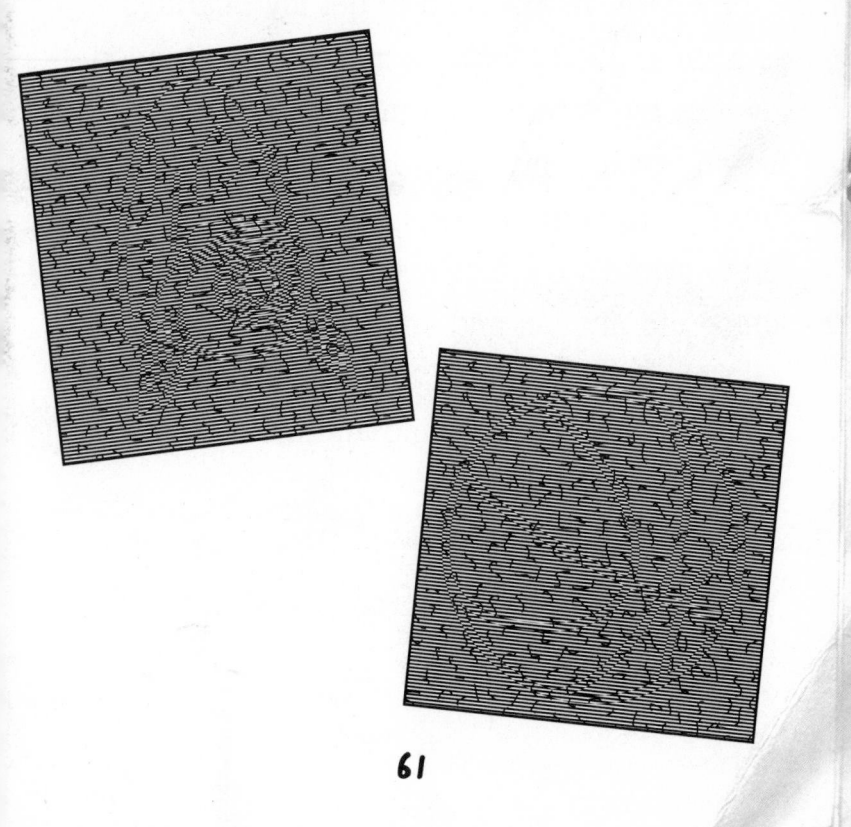

"RARRGGHH!"

I didn't have a second to get my bearings –
as soon as I left Morph, a masked man leaped
towards me, sweeping a massive sword through
the air towards my neck! I ducked and rolled
forwards through his legs, feeling the swish
of the sword's edge over the top of my head. I
jumped to my feet and spun around.

"Stand still, coward!" the man roared.

"I'm not the one fighting an unarmed boy!" I
yelled.

Thankfully I hadn't wasted my time in ancient
Rome – I had learned a ton of fighting techniques

from one of the greatest soldiers of all time, Mark Antony. I had spent years there perfecting my fighting skills, and I had never needed them so much as right now. This masked man had to be Mutex, and that meant I was doomed. The mask made its wearer completely invincible!

Still, there was no point in giving up. At least I could get that sword out of his hands! It was a deadly-looking thing – made of wood, but with razor-sharp metal edges that could have easily taken my head off. I scissor-kicked upwards as he lunged at me, and the sword sailed out of his hand and spun through the air above our heads. As his eyes followed it, I dived at his legs and we both crashed to the dusty ground.

I felt a burning sensation as layers of skin were seared off my legs and arms, but I ignored the pain. Mark Antony had taught me how to focus all my energy on outwitting my enemy. As I struggled to my feet, I saw his face in my mind's eye, and heard his calm, strong voice saying, "Relax into the flow of battle, Will. Never allow your enemy to confuse or frighten you."

"Who are you?" hissed Mutex.

"One that you should not underestimate," I replied.

I realized that we were in the jungle, probably on one of the mountains that were collapsing in King Cocoza's time.

"You appeared out of thin air, like a god!" my opponent said, panting.

"I am here to stop you!" I declared.

"You will never defeat me!" he roared.

He hurled himself at me, and although I tried a defensive tactic, he was too big and strong – I was too small. He smashed me back against the

WILL'S FACT FILE

Dear Adventurer,

If you've already read my Aztec adventures, you should know something about one of the greatest civilizations the Americas have ever seen. But did you know that Aztec priests thought nothing of killing thousands of innocent people every year? Even priests fought in battles. They thought fighting was a way of honouring the gods – plus it was a pretty good way of expanding the empire.

This fact file is packed with lots of cool stuff about the Aztecs. Check out the facts and timeline and then amaze your friends and family with your knowledge.

The Aztecs:

- were ancient people from Mexico.
- were a highly organized society.
- were a bloody-thirsty bunch who thrived through warfare and made human sacrifices.
- built artificial lakes.
- were famous for their agriculture.
- called their capital Tenochtitlan.
- developed a form of hieroglyphic writing.
- had their own calendar.
- built amazing pyramids and temples.
- wore masks, covered in turquoise or shell, to take part in sacred ceremonies and religious sacrifices.
- were a civilization that lasted for just over 200 years.
- eventually fell at the hands of the Spanish conquistadores.

Timeline

1100s
The Aztecs leave their former home in northwestern Mexico.

1325
They settle in Tenochtitlan.

1350
Causeways and canals are built.

1440
The height of the Empire is reached under King Moctezuma (also called Montezuma I).

1487
Dedication of the Great Temple at Tenochtitlan.

1502–1520
Reign of Moctezuma II, or Montezuma II, most famous of the Aztec kings and ninth king of Tenochtitlan.

1517
A comet appears in the sky, believed to be a sign of impending doom.

1519
Spanish conquistadores led by Hernan Cortes land on the Yucatan peninsula in March and arrive at the gates of Tenochtitlan in November.

1520
Assault on the Aztec Empire by Cortes begins.

1521
Fall of Tenochtitlan — the Aztec Empire is destroyed.

1522
Work begins on rebuilding the city by the Spanish as Mexico City, capital of New Spain.

Priests said to settle where an eagle perched with a snake in his mouth.

The beginning
According to ancient legend, the Aztecs left their home sometime in the 1100s AD.
· They wandered for 200 years.
· In about 1341, they found the eagle on the shore of Lake Texcoco (where Mexico City is today).
· The Aztecs founded their capital here, and named it Tenochtitlan.

Tenochtitlan
Tenochtitlan was a great city, with temples, plazas and a marketplace.
· There were 'eating houses', hairdressers and apothecaries.
· In the centre of the plaza was the towering Great Pyramid.
· By the mid 1400s, Tenochtitlan had about 300,000 people, making it the largest city in the world at that time.

Priests performed bloody sacrifices at the top of the Great Pyramid.

Floating islands
The Aztecs built artificial 'floating' islands for agriculture.
· They were made by piling mounds of mud on mats made from reeds.
· They were anchored to the lake bottom by the roots of willow tree
· The islands were used to breed animals and grow food, including maize, avocados, beans and caca beans for making a chocolate d

Farmers carried crops to the market by canoe or by foot.

Trade and merchants

Trading was an important part of life.

- The Aztecs had no metal money.
- In the beginning they simply bartered by exchanging goods.
- As the empire grew, they used the valuable cacao bean as currency.
- Aztec merchants had a class of their own, called pocheta, which was above the common farmers.

The cacao bean was used to buy tools, clothes and gems at markets.

Food

The farmers produced plenty of food for the Aztec people.

- The average Aztec ate twice a day.
- The main meal was taken during the hottest part of the day.
- They regularly ate tomatoes, avocados, tortillas and tamales.
- Only warriors and the wealthy were allowed a chocolate drink made from cacao and maize.

Maize, made into a form of porridge, was the main food source.

Society

In Aztec society, class structure was very important.

- An emperor ruled the Aztecs.
- Then there were the nobles, including priests and warriors.
- Then there were commoners, who carried out manual work.
- At the bottom of society were slaves, who had no rights.

Many commoners were farmers who owned land with a family.

Children

Life could be tough for a child.

- If a child misbehaved he could have cactus spines stuck into him.
- Both boys and girls, even slaves, had to attend school by law.
- Children were taught strict laws of behaviour.
- These included 'Do not complain' and 'Only nobles may carry a fan'

One punishment was to breathe in fumes from a chilli-fuelled fire.

Warriors

The Aztecs believed it was a religious duty for every man to be a warrior.

- A boy's umbilical cord was buried on a battlefield for dedication to war.
- Elite jaguar warriors wore fur costumes and carried wooden clubs.
- Ordinary warriors wore feathered headdresses and primitive armour.
- They used bows, arrows and spears.

The bravest fighters became eagle warriors, decorated with feathers.

Homes

How and where you lived depended on your social status.

- The furniture and huts of the poor were very simple.
- Nobles lived in grand houses.
- By law only nobles' houses could have a second storey.
- Every home had a hearth: a flat disc of hard clay on stones with a fire beneath it.

The poor made do with simple one-roomed huts.

Aztec clothes

Different classes of Aztecs wore different clothing.

Nobles wore cotton clothes and feather headdresses.

It was against the law for common people to wear cotton.

Ordinary folk wore clothes made from maguey cactus fibre.

Men wore loincloths and cloaks. Women wore skirts and tunics.

The Aztecs made a vivid red dye from the cochineal beetle.

Aztec medicine

Aztec apothecaries dished out all sorts of herbal and spiritual remedies.

· The sick were told to say a prayer and make an animal sacrifice.

· Tobacco and plant sap were burned to purify a sick person's house.

· Yellow chillies were recommended for stomach upsets.

· They used steam baths to sweat out evil spirits that caused fevers.

Ground glass was sprinkled on cuts.

Religion and human sacrifice

These were a very important part of Aztec life.

· They honoured their gods by making human sacrifices.

· Sacrificial victims were usually male slaves or prisoners of war.

· In one ceremony to the god Tlaloc, even children were sacrificed.

The Aztecs worshipped hundreds of gods and goddesses.

Crime and punishment

Almost every part of Aztec life was governed by a law.

- Anyone accused of a serious crime was tried at the emperor's court.
- There were no prisons so punishment was swift and brutal.
- Death sentences were common.
- Some minor criminals were put into slavery or exiled.

At local courts, warriors acted as judges.

Fun and games

The Aztecs found time for dance, music and games.

- They danced at religious festivals.
- Music played at human sacrifices.
- The most common instruments were rattles, whistles, trumpets, flutes, copper bells and shells.
- Anyone could play patolli, a board game with bean counters.

The ruling class played tlachtli, a ball game between two teams.

End of an empire

The Aztec empire faltered when the Spanish arrived in 1519.

- Spanish invaders and Aztec enemies marched on Tenochtitl
- Emperor Montezuma was killed and the city destroyed by Herna Cortes and his men in 1521.
- It was the end of the ancient Aztec empire.

Cortes and his men were ruthless searching for land and gold.

rough trunk of a tree and held me there, one arm across my throat.

I stared at the mask that covered his face. It was long and made of gold, with a long slit for the mouth, a breathing hole for the nose and two almond-shaped holes for the eyes. All I could see of my attacker was a pair of fierce, dark eyes.

"You will regret trying to harm me!" he said.

With his free hand he fumbled for something in his waistband, and I saw the gleam of a cruel-bladed knife. I struggled, but it was like a mouse trying to push away an elephant.

"You cannot stop the rise of a new civilisation, stranger," said my defeater.

"Mutex, just think about it for a minute," I croaked, as his arm choked me.

"Mutex?" he bellowed. "Don't you know who I am? Address me by my proper title, peasant! I am Zolton, King of the Triple Alliance!"

"What?" I exclaimed, my voice just a squeak. "You're the King? That's awesome!"

He released his pressure on me a little.

"What do you mean, boy?"

"I mean that if you're the King, I'm not here to fight you, I'm here to help you!"

"Explain yourself!" the King roared.

I thought fast. Right now I was in serious danger of losing my life – I had to think of something to persuade the King that I was on his side.

"I know what your mask does," I said. "I know that it makes the wearer invincible."

I could see his eyes grow narrower behind the mask.

"How could you know that? Only I and my most trusted advisors know that!"

I decided to tell him everything – it was my only hope.

"You saw me appear out of nowhere, right?" I asked. "I am a traveller in time. It's a sort of magic that will be discovered far into your future. I've been sent back by another King – he's got to be your great-great-great-grandson or something. You're in danger! Someone is going to steal your mask – I've come to warn you and to stop it from happening."

The King stared deeply into my eyes. He had a fierce, penetrating gaze.

"Your tale is incredible," said the King slowly. "But to be a great King one must be a good judge of character, and I judge you to be honest."

He stepped backwards, releasing me.

"There are many things in this world that even a King cannot understand," he added.

I rubbed my throat, feeling a wave of relief crash over me. I was in time! I could prevent the robbery! Now that the King was warned, he would stop Mutex from stealing the mask.

"You have to put it somewhere safe," I said. "Have you got a secret hiding place? Somewhere no one could ever find it?"

The King laughed. "I made this mask with my own two hands," he said. "I crafted it using gold and jewels from the mountains of my homeland. I never take it off, and I cannot be defeated while I'm wearing it. Be at peace, time traveller. The mask is safe."

I felt as if a great weight had been lifted from my shoulders. The King had been warned – even if Mutex tried to make friends with him or become a member of his staff, the King would recognize his name.

"You will dine with me tonight," the King said. It was an order, not a request!

"Certainly, Your Majesty," I said, bowing to him. "I am at your service." I know that sounds corny, but I think it's what I was supposed to say!

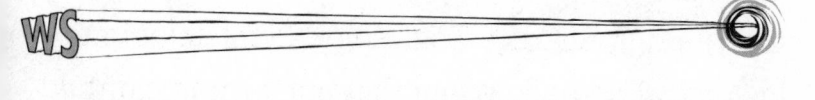

I had come to the early days of the Aztec Empire. The site that would be a great city in King Cocoza's time was now just a collection of homes around a central square. Most of them were just flimsy huts, but there were a couple made of brick. I guessed they must belong to the King.

There was a campfire in the central square, and several men were relaxing around it. I could see women and children working and playing around the huts.

The men scrambled to their feet and bowed when they saw the King. He laughed and waved his hand at them.

"Be seated, be seated!" he said. "We have a guest. This is Will Solvit, and he has brought me vital information. Tonight, we will celebrate his arrival and show him that our people can be joyful as well as war-like!"

The Aztecs settled back around the fire with the King among them. The sun was sinking, and the sound of women singing drifted over from the hut-homes where they were preparing food. Children brought us clay bowls filled with maize, vegetables and meat. The men told stories of war and legends of long-dead heroes. They recited poems about love, and about their gods. Then their wives joined us around the fire, and they all sang together into the early hours of the morning.

The King led me to the little hut where I'd be sleeping, pointing out star formations in the sky as we walked. He told me their names, which were very different from the ones I was used to.

"Goodnight, Will," said the King. "I am very glad you came with your warning."

He smiled and walked away. I lay down on the rough bed, feeling warm and happy.

I should have known the feeling wouldn't last.

I was woken in the morning by a shout.

"Robbers! Thieves!"

I was on my feet and out of the hut almost before I had opened my eyes. A man was standing in the central square, shouting in fury. I didn't recognize his face, but I knew his voice. It was the King.

"What's happened?" I cried, running up to him. "Where's the mask?"

"Will!" he exclaimed. "Someone took it while I was asleep! I must have been drugged – I slept so heavily!"

Another man ran up to the King, panting and wide eyed.

"One of the villagers is missing, my lord," he said. "A man called Mutex."

I stared at the King in horror. Mutex had stolen the mask after all. I had failed!

uh-oh!

CHAPTER SEVEN
THE HEART
OF THE JUNGLE

After a short, jerky trip in Morph, I was back in King Cocoza's time. I felt guilty and sick that I hadn't stopped Mutex. Why hadn't I checked the names of the villagers? Why hadn't I guarded the King all night? Now there was only one thing to do.

I found King Cocoza and told him everything that had happened.

"We have to attack Mutex," I said. "You'll have to put together an army – summon your bravest warriors."

King Cocoza looked very grave.

"We have the finest warriors imaginable, but there are not many of us. All the warriors in the world could not destroy Mutex with the mask."

"Mutex stole the mask by being cunning," I told the King. "If we can get close to Mutex and then distract him with your army, I can try to find a way to steal the mask back."

"Perhaps we should wait and try to build a larger army," the King suggested.

"We haven't got time," I reminded him. "If Mutex does much more mining, your mountains will collapse and your civilisation will be crushed. I . . . I'm sorry, Your Majesty. But this really is our only hope now."

The King rested his hand on my shoulder. "I believe in the prophecy," he said, "and I believe in you. Perhaps all this was meant to be."

I looked down at my feet and hoped that I could live up to his expectations. Whoever told the Aztecs that I was the Master of Time had some serious explaining to do!

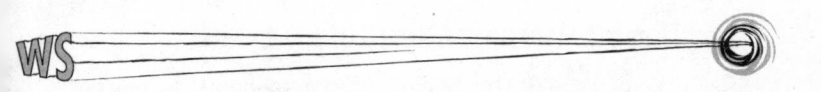

A short time later, the King and I were marching into the jungle at the head of a fearsome army. Now, things were looking pretty desperate and we were heading straight into terrible danger, but I couldn't take my eyes off the warriors. They looked mega-cool in their feathered headdresses and decorated armour. Each warrior was painted and tattooed, and the King looked as if he could destroy cities by himself. I felt really proud to lead them!

As we marched, the King handed me a sword. It was nothing like the heavy metal sword I had been used to in Roman times. This was wooden, very like the sword that the first King of the Aztecs had owned.

"I'm hoping I won't need this," I said.

"So am I," said the King. "But take it . . . just in case."

We trampled deeper and deeper into the jungle, pushing through thick leaves, and stepping over roots as thick as tree trunks. Animals scattered as we marched along. I saw jaguars prowling nearby, watching us – I even saw a silky black-coated jaguar disappearing into the undergrowth. Long, brightly coloured snakes

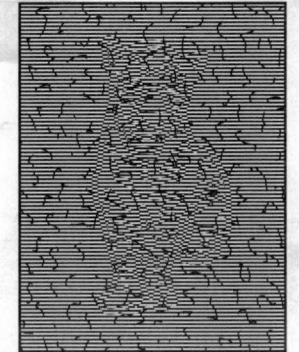

coiled down from trees and slithered through the grass under our feet. The animals I saw reminded me of how Mutex was destroying their homes. If I didn't defeat him, the jungles and the animals of Mexico would be lost.

Suddenly the earth shook and I had to grab hold of a tree trunk to stay upright. Leaves tumbled down from the trees around us, and the warriors looked unsettled. I hung on until the mini earthquake stopped.

"The shakes are getting worse," said the King. "The men are afraid. They fear the wrath of the gods."

I couldn't allow the army to be afraid now. If they ran, I would never get close to Mutex and the mining would bring the mountains crashing down around us.

I swung myself up into the branches of the tree

and looked down on the warriors.

"This shaking is all Mutex's fault," I said. "It's the work of a man, not of a god. But everyone will suffer if we can't stop him. We have to hurry! I know you're all brave and strong, but right now what we need is speed. We have to reach Mutex before the mountain collapses. Don't be afraid! If we stand together, I know that we can stop Mutex and set your children free!"

The Aztecs cheered and shook their spears above their heads. I just hoped that my speech would keep them going until we reached Mutex's secret city!

I jumped down beside the King and we set off again – but this time at double the speed. We were almost sprinting now, racing towards the centre of the jungle. The new city had to be there!

We had been running for over two hours when I saw a small figure sitting on a tree root ahead of us.

"Halt!" I called.

I walked forwards, the King beside me. When we got closer, we saw that it was a little girl. She was crying, and her feet and legs were bleeding.

"Child, have you come from Mutex's city?" asked King Cocoza.

The little girl looked terrified.

"Don't be scared," I said, crouching down beside her. "We're friends – we've come to stop Mutex."

"No one can stop him," said the girl, her voice shaking. "He has this mask—"

"I know about the mask," I said, "and I will stop him."

I sounded mega-confident – if only I was!

"This is the Master of Time," the King told her. "You know the legends, and you must trust them. Now, child, tell us everything you know."

The little girl looked up at me with wide, impressed eyes.

"I escaped," she said. "I've been pretending to be very stupid. The guards weren't watching me this afternoon – they thought I was too stupid to try to escape. I took my chance!"

"What's your name?" I asked.

"Chantico," she replied.

"You have been very brave, Chantico," said the King. "I promise that I will take you to safety. But first I must ask you to do something very courageous for your people. Will you lead us back to the city and show us where Mutex is living?"

I could see that the idea terrified Chantico, but

she didn't hesitate. She stood up and nodded.

"I'll show you the way," she said. "Follow me!"

We mobilized the army again and set off with Chantico in the lead. She led us through a part of the jungle where the leaves seemed to grow thicker and darker with every step.

But then our path opened out into a vast clearing. It was a complete contrast to the beautiful forest – all dirty, dusty and bland. The mountains rose up around us, and there were countless tunnels dotting the area. Everywhere I looked, I saw thin, miserable-looking children carrying piles of stones and earth, pushing massive stones and rolling gigantic logs. Their dirty faces were streaked with tear tracks and many of them were wailing in pain.

King Cocoza was white with fury.

"How dare he do this to my people?" he cried. "When I escaped this place, I vowed that one day I would return and destroy Mutex. Today I fulfil my vow!"

He had his arm around Chantico's shoulder to stop her shaking.

"It's weird that there are no guards on view," I said. "Hey – what's that building in the centre?"

At the heart of the bleak site was a tall, impressive building. Every centimetre of it was adorned with beaten gold and red jewels that glittered dazzlingly. It looked as if it was burning in the sunlight.

"It wasn't here when I was a child," said King Cocoza. "It must be Mutex's palace."

"Then that's where we have to go," I said. "That's where we'll find Mutex, like a spider at the centre of its web."

Mutex!

CHAPTER EIGHT
A BATTLE ROYAL

The King and I spoke to our fierce army of Aztec warriors and explained what we were planning to do.

"We'll storm Mutex's palace and fight past his guards," I said.

"While Mutex's guards are distracted, Will is going to find the mask," King Cocoza added. "So the most important thing is to fight and keep the enemy on the retreat."

"Stay out of sight!" I told Chantico.

Before she could reply or question me (you know what girls are like!) I raced into the palace, unseen by the guards, who were deep in battle with the Aztec warriors. I pelted across an open courtyard and dashed through an archway into the palace itself. Here, the walls were decorated with tapestries and thick with jewels. My footsteps were silent and I realized that I was treading on animal-skin rugs. My skin crawled as I recognized jaguar fur. Mutex obviously cared as little for the animals as he did for the children.

There was a movement up ahead and I peered into the shadows, grasping the hilt of the sword that King Cocoza had given to me.

"Show yourself!" I demanded.

I sounded a lot braver than I felt. But I relaxed when a boy stepped out of the darkness. He was about two years younger than me.

"I'm here to help you," I said. "The guards are fighting our army – we're going to set you free! Just leave the city – you'll be taken to safety. Tell everyone!"

The boy didn't move – he was too shocked! As I looked at him, the ground beneath our feet shook again.

"Go!" I told him. "Mutex's reign is over."

This time the boy nodded and gave me a little smile. Then he raced past me towards the exit. I just hoped that the warriors had managed to defeat the guards!

I ran through hall after hall and explored long, dingy corridors. Every time I saw a child-slave I explained that they were free and told them to leave. I wanted the palace to be empty except for me and Mutex.

I reached a small chamber and paused to look around me. There were no children in here and I was about to walk on when I saw a golden throne at the back of the chamber. It had a large 'M' engraved in it. On the embroidered seat was a small, white envelope, and it had my name on it. Another letter! I raced over and tore it open.

WHAT IS THE MONKEY'S FAVOURITE CHRISTMAS SONG?
JUNGLE BELLS!

YOU'RE VERY CLOSE, BUT THIS PALACE IS A LABYRINTH! TO FIND MUTEX, FOLLOW THESE INSTRUCTIONS:
IN EVERY CORRIDOR, TAKE THE SECOND DOOR ON THE LEFT.
IN EVERY CHAMBER, TAKE THE EXIT NEAREST THE WINDOW.
NEVER GO DOWN A STAIRCASE.

Result! Now I could walk straight to Mutex's hiding place! I still had no idea what I was going to do when I met the masked warrior, but I would have to think about that later. Right now I had to concentrate on the instructions.

The palace was a confusing mass of rooms, corridors and staircases. Without my instructions I would have been lost, but the letter-writer had come to my rescue yet again. I made my way deeper and deeper into the palace, until I came to a staircase that was so narrow I could hardly squeeze up it. It seemed to be getting even narrower, and I would have given up if it hadn't been for the instructions in my letter – there was no way I was going down. I sucked in my breath and pushed myself forwards.

I was astonished to find myself stepping into a wide, oval chamber. There was a single window that looked down on the jungle far below. A man was staring out of it with his back to me. I knew that this had to be Mutex.

I took a deep breath. The moment had arrived at last. I was ready to fight this unbeatable, evil warrior. Against all the odds, I must defeat him and take the mask. I thought about Mark Antony and all the things he taught me. I thought about how I had been in tricky situations before and come out on top. But something was bothering me through all these thoughts. For such a brave, fearsome warrior, Mutex looked kind of . . . small. I mean, he was no taller than me, and he was as thin as Zoe.

Suddenly a voice echoed around the room.

"So you have come at last, Master Solvit."

It was a reedy voice that crackled like dry paper. It gave me the creeps.

"You know why I'm here?" I asked, trying to sound brave.

"You are here to take the mask," said the voice.

I saw his little shoulders shaking and realized that he was laughing. It made me feel angry. How could he stand there laughing when all those children were slaving for him?

"Do you know why I am here?" he asked.

"You're here to fight me," I said. "You want to keep the mask to carry out your evil plans. Well I'm not going to let that happen!"

I pulled out the sword that King Cocoza had given me. I took up a duelling position, and then the figure at the window began to turn around. I stared in amazement and horror.

Mutex was wearing the mask, but that was the only thing that matched my expectations. I had imagined that I would have to face a fearsome warrior, but this was a shrivelled old man! His scrawny arms would not have been able to lift a cup, let alone a sword.

"You're wrong," he said. "I am not here to fight you or to keep the mask from you."

There was a dull thud as the tip of my sword hit the floor.

"What are you talking about?" I asked.

"I have been waiting for you to arrive for many long years," he said. "I want to give you the mask!"

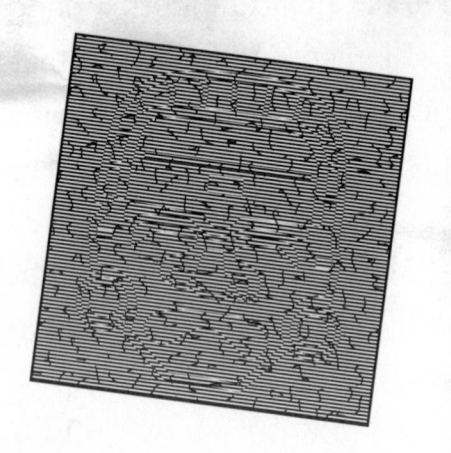

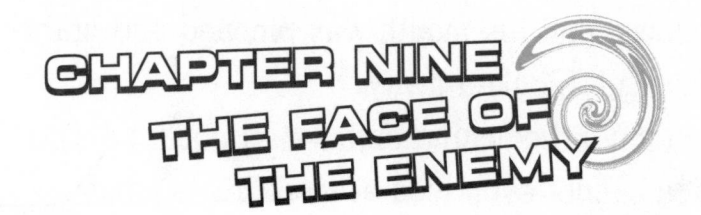

CHAPTER NINE
THE FACE OF
THE ENEMY

I was speechless (and that doesn't happen often.)

What was Mutex talking about? We had raised an army because of his evil ways – why would he just hand over the mask? This had to be a trick. I raised my sword again.

"Will, believe me," said Mutex. "Please, take the mask. It is for you and no one else."

He reached up one withered hand and took off the mask. His face made me shudder. It had lines on top of lines. His eyes had sunk so deep in their sockets that they just looked like black

I'm not sure he can be trusted!

hollows, and his mouth was pinched and crabbed with age. I looked away.

"I am a disgusting sight, am I not?" he said. "You cannot even look at me. This is what lifetimes of evil can do to a man. Pray that it never happens to you, Will Solvit."

He held out the mask to me. I was filled with loathing. The mask was power, and this was what power had done to Mutex.

"I don't want anything to do with the mask," I said. "It'll cause nothing but trouble. You can give it to King Cocoza. He's the rightful owner."

"You are the rightful owner!" hissed Mutex. "One day this mask will save your life!"

"You're crazy," I said, shaking my head at him. "You've gone mental, living here and controlling all those kids. Why did you do it, if it's just going to end like this? What was the point of making

94

them work on your city if you knew you'd never finish it?"

"I need to sit down," said Mutex. "I may be immortal, but I am also a very old man. The mask doesn't stop you ageing."

He placed the mask on the window ledge and lowered himself onto a wooden stool. I kept my sword up – I still wasn't sure that I should trust him.

"I was an ordinary village lad when I stole that mask," he said. "I knew nothing of life. All I knew was that I wanted power. I thought the King was doing things wrong – I thought I would be better than him at ruling the people and growing the empire. It became my dream to have a city built in my honour."

"But what was the point of all the mining?" I demanded.

"My city had to be the best!" he croaked. "I wanted every building to be made of gold and decorated with jewels. And besides, I needed them to find me the right gold and jewels for me to make another mask. I knew that you were coming for this one."

"So you've got two?" I asked.

"No," said the old man. "The children dug and dug, but they never found a single jewel to compare to these on this mask."

"Then how do you expect me to believe

that you want me to take this mask away?" I demanded.

"You may be the Master of Time," Mutex said with a gurgling chuckle, "but you are not the only one who has seen the future. I've met your father."

I dropped the sword with a loud clatter. I felt as if Mutex had hit me around the head with a sandbag. If I'd been Morph I'd have been flashing up a message saying, 'Does Not Compute'. Why would Dad have visited Mutex?

"No." That was all I could think of to say.

"He visited me the night I stole the mask," said Mutex.

My brain was turning into scrambled egg!

"Henry Solvit showed me the future," said Mutex. "He took me to a battle in the stars. Impossible! Wonderful!"

Scrambled egg brain.
Arrgghh!

"Why would my dad take you into the future?" I asked.

"Because he needed me to do something," Mutex told me. "He showed me that great evil was winning the battle. There was only one person who could turn the tide of the battle and overcome the evil."

"Who?" I asked.

"You, Will," said Mutex. "Your father said that if you don't have the mask, then evil would win and it would mean the end of the world."

I closed my eyes, imagining my father talking to Mutex. I could almost hear his voice, explaining about great evil as if he were telling me some dry fact about the Pleistocene period.

"He said I would do many evil things in my lifetime," Mutex continued. "I didn't listen to him. I thought I was going to make everything better."

He gave a laugh that turned into a wet, hacking cough.

"Dad was right though, wasn't he?" I said. "You've done some terrible things."

"He said that I could do one great thing in my life," said Mutex. "I could save the world."

He pushed the mask along the window ledge towards me. My head was hurting. The last thing I wanted was to take charge of some sort of magical object. They're only good for one thing . . . trouble.

But on the other hand, these were my dad's instructions. Was I going to disobey him? What if this was the only way I'd ever get to see him again?

"I'll stop the work," Mutex said. "The children . . . the guards . . . I'll set them all free."

"No more digging?" I asked. "No more cutting

down the jungle?"

"It will all stop," he promised.

"You've destroyed the homes of hundreds of animals."

"I'll build a new place for them to live," Mutex said. "Just take the mask! Please."

I reached out my hand and picked it up. It felt hard and cold. But there was something else there too – a sort of electric spark that jolted into my fingertips.

"All this power," I said. "If my dad's right, one day it'll finally be able to do something good."

I walked to the staircase and then turned to look at the little old man hunched over on the stool.

"Goodbye," I said.

"Good luck," he replied. "I think you're going to need it."

CHAPTER TEN
THE MASTER OF TIME

Outside the palace, I found that King Cocoza and his men had already left. I easily guessed what must have happened. When Mutex gave me the mask, his control over the guards must have disappeared. The battle had stopped and the Aztecs were taking their children home. The King must have known that I had succeeded.

I sat down on a felled tree to think. Whatever I did next had to be the right thing or else I could end up spoiling my dad's plan . . . whatever that might be.

I had to think it through logically. What had I learned so far?

1. I am going to be involved in a battle in the future.
2. The battle will take place in outer space.
3. If the battle is lost, it'll mean the end of the world.
4. I can only win if I have the mask.
5. My dad is involved somehow. That means he's still alive somewhere. I just don't know where.

OK, so that was what I knew. What about the stuff I didn't know?

1. Who had written the legends about me?
2. How had they found out about this Adventure?
3. What was the great evil that I would be battling in the future?

Whoever had written the legends knew an amazing amount of stuff about me. They even knew the exact time and place where I had appeared here.

"Be logical!" I told myself. "Who could know that?"

The more I thought about it, the more impossible it seemed. The legend-writer must:

- Know about my life at home.
- Have seen me arrive.
- Have the ability to time travel.
- Be able to write in my own language.

"I'm being an idiot!" I exclaimed, leaping to my feet. "It was me!"

Of course! I was the only one who could know all those things. I had to get the mask in order to win the battle in the future. That meant that I had to create the legends that would make the Aztecs trust me. I had to go back in time and write the ancient manuscripts. That was why the handwriting had looked so familiar – it was mine!

I put the mask into my backpack and took Morph out. Then I activated the time-travel program. As soon as I stepped inside, I felt the lurching and rolling that meant we were spinning back through time.

With a jerk that nearly knocked me off my feet, Morph stopped and the doors flew open. I shot out, tripped and fell at the feet of the first King of the Aztecs.

"Will!" he exclaimed. "Where have you been? You disappeared! Have you found my mask?"

"Your Majesty," I began . . . and then stopped. How could I possibly explain everything that had happened and was going to happen? I stood up and stared around at the village. Maybe there was still a way that I could save all those kids from slavery and pain. Maybe I could go back in time again and guard the King and the mask. For a moment I imagined how it would feel to fix everything.

"I guess there's been no sign of Mutex?" I asked.

"Someone said that they saw him with another man," said the King. "But we can find no trace of either of them."

I caught my breath. That other man was Henry Solvit – my father! In a flash, all my ideas about messing with time were blown away. Sometimes you can't fix everything. My dad knew that. Mutex was meant to steal that mask, and I was meant to take it from him. I couldn't change that, however hard I tried.

"Listen," I said. "I can't return your mask to you. That's gone for good. But I can make sure that Mutex won't use it to destroy everything you've worked for – and are going to work for. I can't explain it to you; you just have to trust me."

"I told you before," said the King. "I judge you to be honest. Just tell me what you want me to do and I'll make it happen."

The King's servants brought me parchment and pen and ink. It felt weird to write with a sharpened bird feather at first, but I soon got used to it. I wrote the legends of the Master of Time, just as I had read them in the secret room centuries later.

I included every detail that I remembered reading. Then I handed the manuscripts to the King.

"These are the most important pieces of writing in your entire empire," I said. "They're the only things that can stop Mutex and save your people. So you have to guard them and keep them safe. You have to tell every child about them. You have to tell these stories around your campfires at night, and sing

107

songs about them and make up poems."

"They will be passed down through the generations," said the King. "I vow to you that it will be done."

Cool!

We said goodbye and I stepped back inside Morph. But this time there was no shuddering or shaking. We didn't travel anywhere.

"What's the problem?" I asked Morph. "Is there something else I'm supposed to have done?"

I raised my arms questioningly and realized that I was still holding a piece of parchment. In a flash, I knew what to do. I pulled a ballpoint pen out of my bag and wrote a letter.

I really hope Dad sees this! →

Dear Dad,

When you get this, I hope that you know a ton more than I do about what's going on! I'm mega-confused. One minute I'm just the ordinary kid of a famous inventor, and the next I'm a time-travelling Adventurer with both my parents lost in time. It's kind of a lot to take in.

I get that there's loads of stuff you can't tell me, and I'm sure that one day I'll understand everything and we'll all be together again. Adventuring is cool and time-travelling is wicked, but ... I really miss you, Dad.

Take care of yourself and come back home soon.

Luv Will

P.S. If you see Mum, give her my love. Maybe don't tell her about Grandpa's cooking. I'm not sure if she'd approve of some of his recipes.

As I signed my name, Morph started to shake. Green squiggles appeared on the screen and there was a worrying bang. Then the doors swung open. We hadn't moved – we were just outside the village, exactly where we had been before. But it was a different day and a different season. It may even have been a different year.

The only person in sight was a young man, sitting with his back against a tree and looking grumpy.

"Hi," I said, walking up to him. "What's your name?"

"None of your business," retorted the young man.

He stared up at me with arrogance and dislike in his eyes. His skin was smooth and his eyes were bright and blue, but I recognized him.

"You're Mutex," I said.

Mutex scrambled to his feet, staring at me in wonder.

"Are you a prophet?" he asked. "Can you see the future? Will I be rich? Will I be feared?"

I felt really sad as I looked at him. What a weird ambition!

"Yeah," I said eventually. "You'll be all that."

Before he could ask me anything else, I stepped back inside Morph and shut the doors. There was nothing I could do to change the man Mutex would become. I somehow knew that even if he hadn't stolen the mask, he'd have found some other way to fulfil his ambitions. It wasn't the mask that was the problem – it was just the pure evil Mutex had inside him.

"Take me home, Morph," I said.

The four walls of the time machine seemed to spin around me as we hurtled forwards through time. As we got closer to the present, the effects of listening to Mutex's twisted thoughts faded away. By the time we slammed back into my own time, all I could think about was telling Zoe about my Adventures, and finding out how much school I had (hopefully!) missed.

Surely I've been away for at least a week!

CHAPTER ELEVEN
BEEF AND
ICE-CREAM SOUP

As soon as I stepped back into my own bedroom, Morph miniaturized into a tiny model of a time machine. I put it on my desk and grinned at it. We'd done more time travelling together than ever before, this time round. And Morph hadn't misbehaved at all. Maybe I was starting to get the hang of Adventuring!

"You were awesome, Morph," I said.

I slipped my backpack onto the floor and pulled out the mask. Even in this century, the magic of it gave me a faint electric shock.

"You're not staying in here," I told it.

I left my room and made my way up to the attic at the top of the house. I had the key in my pocket and, as I turned it in the lock, I thought of the first time I had entered the attic. I knew so much more now and yet there were still a trillion things to find out.

The door swung open and I walked in. I love the smell of Grandpa's attic. It's dusty and quiet, but it's stuffed with awesome and magical treasures. I bet Grandpa doesn't even remember what half of them are.

I looked up at Titus's sword, displayed on the wall. No one would ever guess that I had marched alongside Titus in ancient Rome, or that I had carried that sword for him! I gazed around, looking for a good home for the mask. It didn't seem to fit with the wooden figurines or the glowing, coloured stones. There was no room for it beside the collection of ma gnif ying glasses, monocles and telescopes.

Suddenly a ray of light sheered through the dusty windowpane and struck an empty space above a marble fire surround. There was no fireplace, but there was an empty nail in the wall that almost seemed to be waiting for the mask.

I hung it up and stepped back. The ray of sun shone onto the mask now, making the jewels sparkle. It would be safe here. I thought of how Grandpa's spy diary had lain up here for years undiscovered. That made me remember the notebook I had started. My diary and clue record contained the details of all my Adventures as well as the clues I had discovered about my parents. I had a lot of new information to fill in!

Back in my bedroom, I wrote a summary of my Aztec Adventures. Then I turned to the page that

I had entitled *CLUES* and read it through again.

1. I will find one parent before I find the other.
2. Neither of them is where I left them.
3. The Partek said that my dad is in a place where I will never find him, but as they are human-hating cat-shaped aliens I'm taking it with a pinch of salt.
4. Mum and Dad made a time machine that took them to the Stone Age.
5. Mum left Dad behind in the Stone Age and went off somewhere in the time machine.
6. Dad got into a Partek spaceship.
7. Mum is stuck somewhere between the Stone Age and the present.
8. I should look for Mum in the past.
9. I should look for Dad in the future.

Now I could add a new clue!

10. Dad sent me a message that I am going to have
to fight against a great evil. The battle will take
place in outer space. I'll need the Aztec mask to
defeat the evil.

I read through the clues about ten times, but I
couldn't figure out what was going on or what I
should do next. I threw the diary onto my desk,
pulled out my SurfM8 and messaged Zoe.

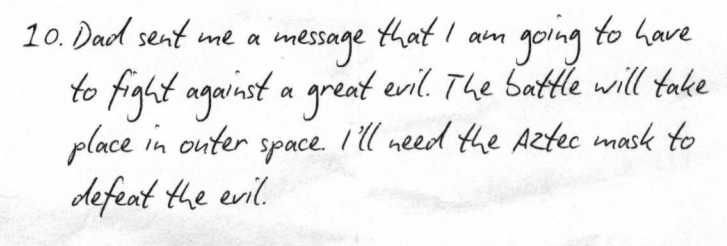

SingaporeSista: I'm nt doing yr homewk 4 u!

Wilz: Wot r u tking abt? How long hve I been gone?

SingaporeSista: No way! U had the Adventure alrdy?

Wilz: Y, how long hs it been?

SingaporeSista: Abt 2 mins, LOL.

Wilz: No way! I missed no schl?

SingaporeSista: Ha ha u hav to live lk a normal kid 4 once!

Wilz: Cnt wait 2 tell u abt the Aztec Adv. Mega-weird!

SingaporeSista: Any news on yr parents?

Wilz: Yep, tell you at schl 2moz.

SingaporeSista: Cnt wait! C u there!

I turned off the SurfM8 and looked at my diary on the desk again. I had a feeling that I had enough clues to figure out what was going on, but my brain just wasn't making the connections. I wished that I knew what my special Adventurer skill was. Every Solvit seemed to have one, so why couldn't I discover mine? I didn't seem to be brilliant at anything in particular – not like Dad. Even Grandpa had once been a skilled spy. I reached for his spy diary and opened it at a random page.

30th September, 1951

There are so many things that I don't understand! Every time I think I know about something, it changes and surprises me and I have to start all over again. Is this what the life of an Adventurer is like? It's so frustrating.

But it is also wonderfully exciting!

"You were right, Grandpa," I said aloud. "I'll try to always remember that, no matter what happens."

Just then I heard Grandpa's voice, calling me from downstairs.

"Where are you, young Henry?" he shouted. "This beef and ice-cream soup won't last forever, you know. You can go on your Adventure anytime, but this is really important!"

I couldn't help but grin. That was another kind of time travel – reading the young Grandpa's diary and then hearing him as an old man!

"OK, Grandpa!" I yelled back. "I'm coming!"

I ran downstairs and found Plato waiting for me at the bottom. He ran around in a frenzy of excitement.

"What's up with you?" I asked, kneeling down to rub his ears. "Hasn't Stanley taken you for your walk yet?"

Stanley is Grandpa's chauffeur and odd-job man. He doesn't say much, but he's awesome. I reckon Grandpa's enormous old house would fall down around his ears if it weren't for Stanley!

"What's that in your mouth?" I asked Plato.

He had something clamped between his jaws. I tried to pull it out, but he thought it was a game. He did some play-growling and then started a tug of war.

As soon as my fingers touched it, I knew that it was an envelope. It had to be another letter for me!

"Plato, drop it!" I said in my

Soooooooo annoying!

122

sternest voice. "Drop!"

Plato obviously thought that this was all part of the hilarious game. He made a huffing sound that was his version of laughing.

"Plato, I mean it!" I said. "Drop that letter right now!"

Wagging his tail, Plato backed away from me towards the kitchen. I followed him, holding out my hand and trying to coax the letter out of him.

Now, usually I take all the proper precautions when Grandpa's trying out a new recipe on me. A nose clip, a pair of gloves and a packet of indigestion tablets are standard. But at that moment all I could think about was getting my letter off Plato, and I walked into the kitchen without any kind of protection at all.

KABLAM! The smell hit me like an anvil between the eyes. I staggered sideways, my throat and nose filled with the bitter smell of burned beef and ice-cream soup. Through my tear-filled eyes I saw Plato in the corner of the room, helpless with sneezes. Grandpa had used way too much pepper. Plato gave a sneeze that raised his front paws off the floor, and the letter shot out of his mouth and into the air. I jumped up and caught it just before it landed in the soup tureen.

"Back in a sec, Grandpa!" I gasped.

I dashed out of the house and sat on the front step, gulping down fresh air as I ripped open the envelope.

WHAT DO DUCKS HAVE FOR LUNCH?
SOUP AND QUACKERS!

WELCOME HOME!
YOUR AZTEC ADVENTURE WAS A COMPLETE
SUCCESS. YOU DID EVERYTHING AND MORE THAN
WAS EXPECTED OF YOU.

I looked at the statues of my ancestors that lined Grandpa's drive. They were shining in the evening light, and I wondered if maybe one day, there might be a statue of me there. I looked down and read the letter again. My next Adventure was going to take place in the future. What was going to happen to me? Was I about to 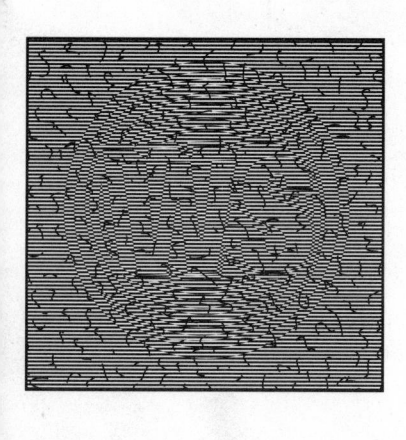 battle the great evil that Dad told Mutex about? Judging by the letter, I was about to find out!

OTHER BOOKS IN THE SERIES